Pee O'Clock

The Imaginary World Of A Historically Adjacent, Children's Book Author

Mark "Dr. Maddog" Donnelly, PhD.

RPSS Publishing - Buffalo, New York

drmaddog@hotmail.com

Pee O'Clock - Perfect Bound

ISBN: 978-1-956688-61-0

Printed in the United States of America

10 9 8 7 6 5 4 3 2 1

RPSS Publishing - Buffalo, New York

This book is dedicated to

Saint Prostate of Perpetual Urgency

and the Brotherhood of

the Midnight March

CONTENTS

PEE
O'CLOCK

Welcome to Pee O'Clock

Every man eventually hits that borderline-mystical stage of life when his bladder starts speaking with more authority than his dreams. Mine began whispering sometime in my sixties–then shouting. Gone were the blissful nights of uninterrupted sleep. In their place arrived the sacred and unpredictable hours of Pee O'Clock: 1:47, 3:03, 4:00 a.m.–each marked by the unmistakable revelation that my bathroom was calling more insistently than destiny ever had.

What began as an inconvenience soon evolved into a ritual, attended by a decidedly unqualified board of advisors: a homicidal cat, a broken swizzle stick promoted to coffee-stirrer, and a sack spider who lives in my coffee machine. Together they function as both my pre-dawn focus group and the only socially acceptable explanation for talking to myself before sunrise. Somewhere in that odd fellowship between the hiss of the coffee pot and the creak of an aging floorboard–I found not just company, but purpose.

With this unlikely committee at my side, Dr. Maddog barrels into the question of how to resist retirement with heroic stubbornness and reinvent himself long after the world assumes he should be slowing down.

This book explores the "evening-side of morning"–those shadowy hours when most of humanity is still asleep and imagination slips in through the cracks left by insomnia. It's the chronicle of a chronologically gifted man who transformed a lifetime of past skill sets into becoming a relatively okay children's book author.

Call it a faux memoir, a parody, or a coffee-fueled confession. Whatever it is, it's the honest truth: I handed my sanity over to caffeine years ago, my mornings are populated by creatures no sensible adult would conjure, and somehow, through all of it, I remain the luckiest, most wide-awake man alive.

The Evening-Side of Morning

My name is Dr. Maddog. No one of any real importance actually calls me by that name. Still, it has been my email address since the invention of the Interweb. It was a silly college nickname that I hoped would stick, but no such luck. It's now my pen name and the avatar I use for the cookbooks I write. By hiding behind this canine persona, I figure people will blame the dog if any recipes go south.

It's zero dark thirty, with the emphasis on dark. It will be a couple of hours before the clouds replace the stars and the tsunami of endless phone, text, and email interruptions from needy students begin. It's not that many centuries ago that this is the same time I would be rolling into the house. It was plenty of time to change my shirt, brush the more obvious teeth, and head to teach class. Now that I'm grayer and the same age as old people, it's when I get up every day.

Waking up this early is an annoying habit. They, whoever they are, say the early bird gets the worm. Rising before the birds and the worms have had a chance to hit the snooze button is my quiet time for reflection, imagination, and pathological creativity. I, unfortunately, sleep like a baby, waking up every couple of hours with a critical need to pee. This schedule is part of my "what the heck" productivity plan. Since I'm already up, I might as well grade some papers.

Every morning begins with the vague, ghostlike silhouette of me perched at the edge of my bed, illuminated only by the soft, judgmental glow of my CNN nightlight–the world's dimmest, and yet somehow most opinionated, beacon. I sit there for a while, not quite awake, not quite asleep, occupying that mysterious state where time has no meaning and the floor feels ten miles away. There's always a long windup before I stand because, at my age, you don't rush these transitions. Sudden movements are how headlines happen.

Before attempting verticality, I conduct my mandatory morning preflight check. I wiggle my toes to confirm they still report for duty, rotate my ankles to see whether they object, and take inventory of everything that snaps, pops, or crackles. If the noises stay below breakfast-cereal volume, I deem myself nominal. Then comes the crucial moment of waiting for gravity to take full hold—because trust me, starting the day before your organs settle is a rookie mistake.

Once cleared for takeoff, I begin my zombie shuffle toward the kitchen, drifting by way of the bathroom like a confused specter. The room is so dark I swear it achieves a color beyond black—something like "midnight with an attitude." I'll continue to call it black until they invent a darker color.

At precisely 2:47 a.m.—which all reputable urologists recognize as Pee O'Clock—my brass twin-bell alarm clock whispers its judgmental little brrring and I shuffle down the hall like a man reenacting the Erie Canal, all locks and slow gates.

I used to believe I was unique in my nocturnal bathroom pilgrimages—two, three, sometimes four times a night. Surely, across the country, other old men are shuffling through their hallways. A retired teacher in Des Moines. A widower in Phoenix. A grandfather in Florida, tiptoeing past seashells.

Then I discovered there's actually a secret society. Not the Masons, although I belong to them too. We're like Masons, only with smaller bladders and worse boxers. It's a lodge that doesn't advertise, but everyone eventually joins.

We're the Brotherhood of the Midnight March. We rise, we shuffle, we flush-alone but together. We don't have a secret handshake, because that would be kinda gross, but we do have a patron saint – St. Prostate of Perpetual Urgency.

We don't meet formally, but there's a knowing nod exchanged at the diner, the barbershop, or in the plumbing aisle at Home Depot. Conversations go something like this:

"Three times last night."

"Ha! Amateur. I did five."

"I don't even bother getting back under the blankets anymore. I just nap on the edge of the bed like a cat."

It's not shame—it's solidarity. These men compare notes like marathon runners. One swears by cutting off coffee after 3 pm (blasphemy), another claims cranberry juice is the secret, and one simply shrugs: "The bladder wants what it wants."

I've accepted it as a brotherhood ritual, a badge of seniority. Forget bowling leagues or book clubs—this is the real Club. Dues are paid in sleep deprivation and a well-worn path to the bathroom.

At our age, it's not insomnia. It's the bladder alarm clock. And it never hits snooze."

Daisy - Feline Assassin

Daisy, part cat, and part furry assassin, provides the midnight march obstacle course. When she's not trying to suffocate me by sleeping on my face, she darts between my legs with each step toward the kitchen/bathroom to test my agility.

Daisy always pretends to be starving, but the second I fill her bowl, this over-pampered brat turns up her nose and saunters away. The only reason I tolerate this is because when calculated in cat years, we're both about the same age.

Let me begin by saying I love my cat. I really do. I picked her out at the shelter. Or rather, she picked me—a little tortoise shell-colored puffball with deep amber eyes, a crooked tail, and a purr like a rusty lawnmower. Her name is Daisy. I named her that because I'm a creative genius with a PhD. and a crippling fear of commitment. Besides, it was the name on her cage at the shelter.

It took exactly three weeks after I brought her home for me to realize: Daisy is trying to kill me.

Now, I'm not saying she's possessed or anything, although I wouldn't be surprised if she had a direct line to Satan's WhatsApp. I'm saying she is a feline agent of chaos with murder in her heart and fur in her claws.

It started subtly. Every morning, without fail, Daisy would dart between my legs as I zombie-walk to either make or release coffee. Now, a lesser mind might think, "Aw, she's just excited to see me." No. Daisy timed her sprints like a NASCAR pit crew.

One morning, I lost my footing, flailed like an inflatable tube man, falling face-first into the potted fern I keep forgetting to water.

Daisy stood on the counter, tail swishing, eyes narrowed, her expression unmistakable:

"Almost."

THE COFFEE FEEDBACK LOOP

I would hope no one believes I'm naturally this intense.

Coffee is my rescue from sleep. As a lifelong, card-carrying java junkie, coffee rules my day.

I'm always hoping for a drum roll or a few bars of "Fanfare for the Common Man" when it's time for the start of the morning coffee ritual: the sacrificial grinding of the beans, the filling of the water, and the all-important selection of the day's mug. The cup selection is a process requiring deep meditation.

I stand before my vast array of ceramic options, arms crossed, considering. At last, I settle a chipped cup that bears the faded slogan, "This meeting could have been an email". It is the vessel most spiritually aligned with today's brew. Picking the wrong mug can really mess up your day. Always choose carefully. The fate of humanity may depend on it.

I approach coffee the way a heart surgeon approaches an open chest cavity –with reverence, precision, and absolutely no tolerance for amateurs. My morning ritual is less about caffeine and more about ceremony. The beans must be whole, ethically sourced, preferably roasted by monks in the mountains of Peru, and ground only moments before brewing – "so the flavor doesn't evaporate into the moral void of the universe."

I don't "make" coffee; I engineer it. The water temperature must weigh-in at precisely 202 degrees, measured with a digital thermometer. I once dismissed my French press for "underperformance" and I keep my filters organized by thickness and absorbency – "like surgical gloves, but for taste."

And heaven help the fool who offers me decaf. It's "a betrayal of science and soul," and once lectured a Barista for calling it coffee at all.

For me, coffee isn't a drink. It's a religion – and I'm both high priest and devoted disciple.

THE SUSPENSE OF THE BREWING BEAST

A coffeemaker does not simply brew. No—this is theater. From the first gurgle, it becomes a Hitchcock film in your kitchen.

It starts with the low hum—like a villain clearing his throat in the shadows. Then the sputtering begins: pffft, glug-glug, wheeze—each sound a cliffhanger. Is it brewing… or dying? Is this the day it finally explodes and redecorates the ceiling in Peruvian Roast?

The steam hisses like a snake plotting something terrible. The pause between burbles stretches into unbearable silence. Has it stopped? Is it finished? Or is it only waiting… waiting to strike?

And then—BAM! The final eruption—a bubbling roar worthy of an angry volcano. The carafe trembles. The counter vibrates. I lean in, eyes wide, whispering: "Don't you dare quit on me now."

At last, the pot falls silent. The coffee is ready. This audience of one exhales. Curtain down. Standing ovation.

Then comes the most dangerous moment: the first sip. Too early, and I'll scorch my tongue into uselessness. Too late, and the day has already outpaced you. Somewhere in that steaming middle ground lies salvation, clarity, and the faint hope that maybe today I'll finally remember where I left my keys.

At coffee shops, they joke that I have a little coffee with my cream. I prefer to think of it as slightly darkening my milk. It's not a culinary choice - I'm old and have a woossie stomach.

My first cup is solely to prime the pump and build my strength to have a second. The next cup pumps the sunshine into my smile, and the third and fourth are to sharpen my trademark snark. For the sake of polite conversation, my friends say I should always stop at cup number two.

In truth, coffee doesn't just wake us up—it forgives us. It forgives the cranky, pre-caffeinated version of ourselves that snapped at the toaster, yelled at Wolf Blitzer, and muttered about quitting civilization.

The Pee O'clock Coffee Club

The once-quiet hour that used to belong solely to me–my sacred window of pre-dawn solitude–has slowly evolved into something far more chaotic, far more ridiculous, and, against all better judgment, far more beloved. There was a time when 4 a.m. was my sanctuary, a place where I could sit in monk-like silence, letting my mind float in that delicate balance between consciousness and the gentle art of staring blankly into the middle distance. I convinced myself it was "deep thought," though if the universe had held a mirror to my face, I suspect it would have labeled the expression "system reboot in progress."

Back then, the world was still. The coffee pot hissed like an old friend with secrets. Even the refrigerator hummed with the steady wisdom of a seasoned philosopher. Princess Laura and the Queen Mother slept soundly upstairs, their royal snores drifting faintly down the hallway like distant horns announcing peace across the kingdom. The cat had completed her dawn patrol–three laps of the house, two dramatic pauses, and one blood-curdling yowl for no apparent reason. She's ceremonially demanded her breakfast, and was already curled in a loaf of judgment at the edge of the table.

And me? I had accepted long ago that the universe wakes me at 4 a.m. for a reason. Not a profound reason, mind you–just a reason. Some people rise early to write novels or train for marathons or seize the day. I get up because my bladder schedules mandatory staff meetings.

Which is precisely when my Pee O'Clock Coffee Club convenes.

We gather faithfully each morning at the kitchen table, a council of mismatched personalities bound together by caffeine, insomnia, and mutual confusion about why we are awake at this ungodly hour. It is less of a club and more of a spontaneous focus group evaluating the day before the day even knows it has started.

Some people have imaginary friends. I, however, have an entourage of real objects with imaginary backstories—a far more dignified alternative to holding long conversations with myself. My companions are peculiar, yes, but at this hour, with no witnesses and no adult supervision, they've become my chosen family.

There's Daisy the silent assassin, who sits on the table like a furry gargoyle, tail twitching with quiet disapproval. She believes herself to be the Chaircat of All Committees and has veto power over any motion involving food, warmth, or attention.

Then there's DH, the broken swizzle stick formerly from the Playboy Club in Chicago I once rescued from a junk drawer. Most people would've thrown it out. I, however, reinvented it as a coffee stirrer and granted it emeritus status after years of honorable service. It doesn't do anything anymore, but its presence is inspirational—proof that we all deserve a second act, even if we're old, broken, and bent in the middle.

The newest member is Running Ralph, a hyperactive sack spider. He's a cheerful maniac who has taken up residence inside the coffee machine. He scurries about as if he's late for a very important meeting—which, in fairness, he probably is. He contributes nothing to the conversation but enthusiasm, which is more than I can say for many humans I've met.

Together, we form the Pee O'Clock Coffee Club: an unlikely coalition of man, beast, utensil, and arachnid. We sip coffee, contemplate existence, and hold unofficial kitchen-table focus groups on topics ranging from "Why am I awake again?" to "Is the refrigerator humming in E-flat this morning?"

They are unconventional. They are absurd. They are undeniably strange.

And yet, somehow, these odd companions—this kitchen-table cast of misfits—have become the tiny, ridiculous family that greets each new day with me. Before the world wakes, before the rush begins, before Princess Laura descends the stairs demanding to know why the cat looks smug, they are here.

Naturally, these companions concern visitors.

Not because of what they are, but because of who they've become.

Old people—my demographic cohort—have a reputation for talking to themselves. Mumbling while they walk. Holding full conversations while searching for their keys. Offering opinions to toasters. It's all very dignified.

But I say giving backstories to inanimate objects is simply practice. Practice for stretching the imagination. Practice for creative thinking. Practice for crafting narratives grand enough to capture the attention of students.

And frankly, it seems less psychotic than answering my own questions out loud.

So yes, I give them personalities. The spider is a jittery barista-in-training for the Olympics. The swizzle stick is a retired showbiz legend. The cat is plotting a household coup. And me? Well, I'm the slightly bewildered professor and chairman of this kitchen-table circus, conducting 4 a.m. meetings because my bladder insists on waking me up at ungodly hours.

If anyone asks, this is my own strange method of staying creative, engaged, and marginally sane in the predawn quiet.

Even though sanity may have become more of a suggestion than a certainty, this probably isn't evidence of mental decline.

It's research.

RUNNING RALPH

There's my friend Running Ralph. Turning on the coffee maker is his alarm clock. It's his cue to jump into action, instantly going from zero to sixty as he sprints a lap or two around the coffee pot and then the length of the countertop a few times before returning to his room to rest. For a tiny yellow sack spider, this dude can make all those little legs really move. He claims sleeping beside the caffeine delivery system has nothing to do with his extraordinary speed.

Ralph has hundreds of siblings and claims they're all just as handsome as he is. He spends his daylight hours stalking and eating microscopic bugs that live on the windowsill over the sink.

Now that I'm growing miniature pots of herbs like parsley, basil, and rosemary there, he says the kitchen deserves a 3-star Michelin rating. He's promised to share some recipes with me for my next cookbook.

DH

Enter the other member of my pre-dawn cohort – Deaf Hugh, or DH, as his friends call him. Hugh is an extraordinary old soul with a storied past. More than a mere coffee stirrer, he was once the face of the famed Playboy Club.

In his youth, DH's dynamic black silhouette became the logo of a chain of international nightclubs and resorts owned by his namesake, Hugh Hefner. His first job was at the Playboy Club, which opened in Chicago in 1960.

For many years, Hugh sat on the piano of Sam Distefano. Sam would use Hugh like a conductor's baton when he led the 32-piece house orchestra. Hugh was skillfully waved for performers such as Dean Martin, Sammy Davis Jr., Tony Bennett, Wayne Newton, and dozens of other superstars whose names will only impress you if you're really old.

Hugh loves to tell the story about the night a close-up magician who worked the Club Room made him disappear, only to suddenly reappear firmly wedged in a Playboy Bunny's cleavage. His memories of the waitress who would eventually become Playboy magazine's Miss July are crystal clear. In fact, they get clearer and more detailed each and every time he tells the story.

In 1991, the Playboy Club chain became defunct, and the next few years became a blur of thrift stores and silverware drawers. Hugh eventually surfaced in a basement bar in the home of Chet and Terry, an old Polish couple whose last name he could never pronounce or spell. They lived in a middle-class suburb of Buffalo, New York.

To fit in, Hugh quickly changed his loyalties from supporting Da Bears to a table-crushing, condiment-squirting Buffalo Bills fan. The pine-paneled bar he now worked was ground zero for many weekends of socially lubricating family and friends. It wasn't the glitz and celebrity of Chicago, but these were happy times, and it was good to be employed again.

With the sad passing of Chet in 2015, the bar and all the assorted bar hardware, like Hugh, were packed up by his daughter (and my wife), Princess Laura, and taken to our house.

Fortunately, this is far from the end of this story. Even though Princess Laura and I are not drinkers, Hugh was repurposed from a cocktail swizzle stick to a professional coffee stirrer. Now scuffed up and missing both his ears, broken off during all the transporting around, he's thrilled to be working and a vital part of the family. DH brings some exceptional skill sets to his new profession. Because he is ambidextrous, he can stir both clockwise and counterclockwise.

Although unable to hear and without hands to sign, Hugh has become a fantastic lip reader. Being old-school and proud to be thoroughly politically incorrect, he prefers the term deaf over hearing impaired or hearing challenged. He likes to brag that even without ears, he can hear better than most other coffee stirrers. It comes from his years of working behind a bar. Being an attentive and sympathetic listener really adds to the tip jar.

Working for teetotalers has admittedly been a challenge for DH. There's a world of difference between dodging ice cubes in a cocktail's frozen plunge and the near-boiling hot tub of a cup of coffee. Fortunately for Hugh, because of his advancing age, the parts of him most sensitive to temperature are missing in action. I often place some tiny cocktail umbrellas in my morning brew to try to ease his transition. He's not impressed, but it adds a little class to the joint.

DH now lives in a wooden block that houses a family of German knives, all named Henckel. He shares a slot with a 10-inch chef's knife that doesn't speak a syllable of English. Fortunately, the Henckels are all great listeners. They haven't a clue what DH is endlessly bragging about, but they somehow appreciate the joy in his voice and the twinkle in his plastic eye while he talks.

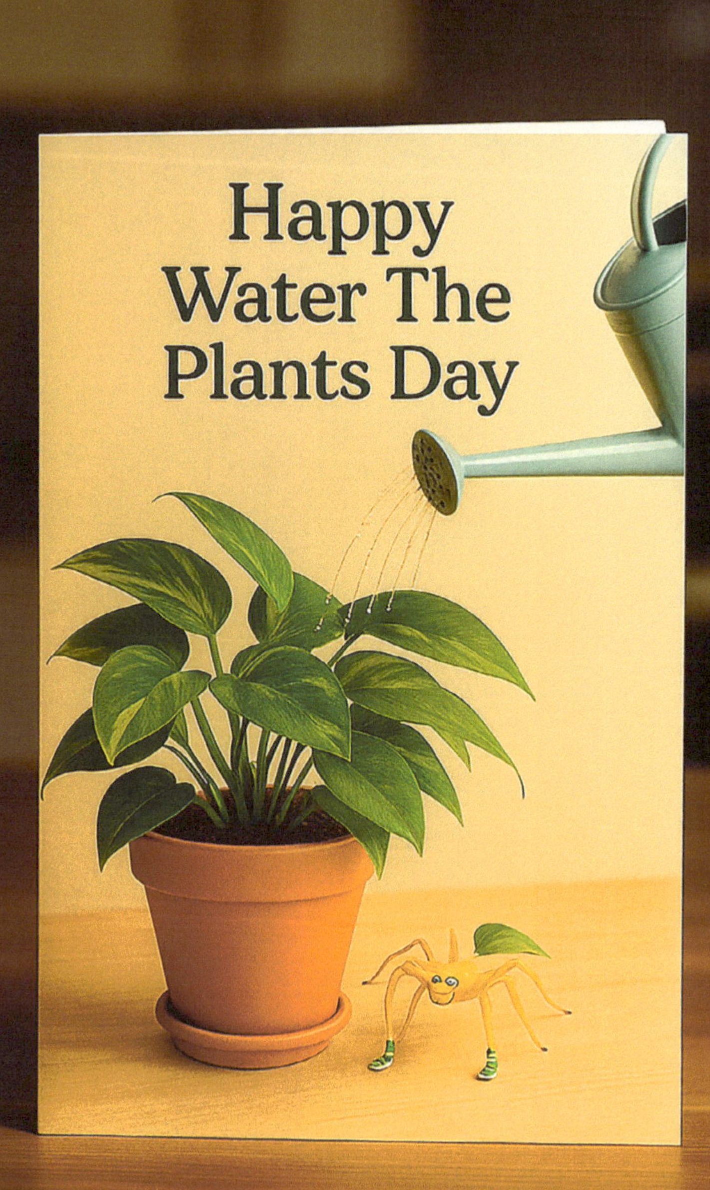
Happy
Water The
Plants Day

JUST ANOTHER DAY

Today is sure to be like any day because they're all pretty much the same. My family claims it's my birthday, but that's impossible because I swear I just had one just last week.

When I say that all days are the same, there are, of course, exceptions. Every Tuesday is "Happy Water The Plants Day." One of my life's greatest disappointments is that the celebration I originated never caught on as a Hallmark card-level holiday. I've even designed my own cards to try to jumpstart a populist movement.

The other red-letter day is Friday morning. I dramatically race to take out the trash each week before the garbage truck arrives. It wouldn't be such a big deal if I had taken it out the night before, like everyone else in the neighborhood. It adds a bit of extra spice to the end of each week.

While we may sound boring, this morning crew isn't without its occasional adventure. A couple of times a year, Deaf Hugh goes missing because he is mistaken for something disposable or discarded because he's broken. The 911 operator is no longer amused. After a thorough manhunt, usually ending in dumpster diving, we are all reunited. We celebrate with coffee sporting tiny umbrellas.

About a month ago, my 95-year-old mother told me with great pride that she had just killed a spider in the kitchen, and she poured its lifeless remains down the sink. I was devastated. Though tiny, Running Ralph had a supersized role in my pre-dawn circle. His frenetic antics had been a great source of entertainment, and his resilience served as an important role model. I spent most of that afternoon arranging a memorial service and preparing to hand out black armbands.

The following day, at its usual appointed time, I turned on the coffee machine. To my delight, a very undead Ralph popped out, did his daily laps and sprints, and returned to his miniature home as though nothing had happened. This whole adventure was, fortunately, just a matter of mistaken identity. It was actually Bob, one of Ralph's hundreds of identical cousins, who met this unseemly demise. We held a funeral in Bob's honor anyway. May he rest in peace.

As proof that coffee solves everything, our daily group discussion is the highlight of each morning. It's incredible how easily we can solve all the world's issues over a single cup of Joe.

I once read that the White Queen says she's believed as many as six impossible things before breakfast. We sent her an open invitation to join our group. No response to date.

We discuss highbrow intellectual topics such as Middle East peace, corporate gains, Coke vs. Pepsi, Wordle streaks, and the temperature at which it's necessary to wear socks and long pants.

To facilitate a civil conversation, we each raise our hand to speak next. Ralph, by the nature of his multiple arms, tends to dominate the conversation completely. By contrast, DH, lacking arms altogether, always feels slighted and consistently breaks this rule.

Daisy, the cat, occasionally tries to join in. She, unfortunately, knows only one word, said with multiple inflections. Her topics only focus on eating, sleeping, and chasing the laser dot.

GET
SHIT
DONE

Princess Laura's Kingdom

While I am busy at four in the morning conducting bladder diplomacy, my wife – Princess Laura is sleeping soundly in preparation for her real job. Unlike me, she has a kingdom that requires order, patience, and infinite stamina: a high school classroom filled with children from every corner of the globe.

She is still, after all these years, a dedicated teacher of English to immigrant students. Each September she receives a new collection of faces, each with a different story, each speaking a different language, and all of them thrust into the chaos of American adolescence without a dictionary. Some kids come from refugee camps, some from big cities, some from villages where electricity is a rumor. They arrive scared, tired, and hopeful.

And then they meet her.

I call her "Princess" not because she wears a tiara (though she deserves one) but because she rules with a steady hand and a kind heart. She waves her dry erase marker like a scepter, her voice firm but encouraging, her classroom equal parts sanctuary and training ground. The magic is not just that she teaches English, but that she teaches survival. Her students don't just learn verbs and vocabulary; they learn how to order lunch in the cafeteria, how to fill out a bus pass form, how to navigate the labyrinth of teenage life in a strange new language.

At dinner, she tells me their stories. The girl from Myanmar who taught herself the alphabet in three weeks. The boy from Somalia who translated jokes into English and had the entire class laughing. The Ukrainian twins who didn't say a word for months but soaked up everything, then one day started speaking in full sentences as though they had been waiting for the curtain to rise.

Her job is exhausting, and yet she loves it. She thrives on the small victories, the moment a student raises their hand and gets it right, the day an essay arrives scribbled with awkward but heartfelt words like, "I happy here. Teacher nice."

I sometimes wonder what her students think of me, the eccentric husband who writes about murderous cats and bathroom routines. To them, she must look like the most patient woman on earth, carrying a torch of clarity through a fog of confusion. And she is.

While my mornings are filled with caffeine-fueled chaos, her mornings are filled with lesson plans, vocabulary lists, and an iron determination to make sure every kid has a fighting chance.

She may not call it a kingdom, but I do. And in that kingdom, she is both queen and champion, proving every day that words matter, that kindness transcends language, and that even in a room where twenty different tongues collide, one voice of encouragement can be understood by all.

And so, while I stumble through my strange little world, she strides through hers with grace. She is my Princess, and her crown is invisible but undeniable.

Dawn's Crack

Before long, the dog next door barks, and there is the familiar thump on the porch of the daily newspaper. A brief look out the window shows where the sky has been eating the darkness and coloring it with the whole box of Crayons. This is the old man version of the child of morning, rosy-fingered dawn. It's all part of Homer's formula that things have an eternal, infinitely repeatable presence. Different things will happen every day, but dawn always appears, always with rosy fingers, and always early.

The bliss of quiet is beginning to break with the realization that it's nearing the moment for starched shirts, tight shoes, and the appearance of rational thought.

It's that time again to open my eyes the rest of the way and dive headfirst into the new day's journey with all the chaos and opportunity it will surely bring. I can confidently muddle forward, knowing that the last threeish cups of coffee have put enough of a bounce in my step and a smile on my face. Zero dark thirty will arrive all too soon again. Hopefully, tonight we can finally resolve the Coke versus Pepsi debate.

By 7:30, I'm still not quite yet human but it's time for this boxer-wearing philosopher and self-appointed president-for-life of the Pee O'Clock Coffee Club to gavel in a new day. By unanimous decree, civilization may continue—at least until tomorrow's meeting.

I rise, robe trailing like a superhero cape in retirement. Glasses on, remaining hair mostly tamed, ready to face the most frightening prospect of all: the absurdities of the "real world".

By the time the sun comes up, I've already lived a whole other life.

Then comes the awkward moment when the rest of the world begins its workday.

Neighbors put on ties, grab briefcases, and commute to respectable jobs with direct deposits. My wife heads into her own carefully ordered schedule, shaking her head as I refill my coffee cup for the fourth time. And me? I wander to the car to drive to campus.

THE ART OF HIGHER EDUCATION

(Mostly Lowered Expectations)

At precisely 7:55 a.m., I shuffle into my lecture hall – coffee in one hand, existential dread in the other. My students, most of whom looked like they'd rather be anywhere else (preferably horizontal), barely looked up from their glowing rectangles of infinite knowledge. It was Intro to Marketing, but for me it's more like "Intro to Herding Cats With Wi-Fi."

"Good morning, scholars," I proclaim, with the enthusiasm of a man reading his own eulogy.

A few mumbled "mornings" floated up from the rows, though it was unclear whether they came from the living or the sleep-walking.

I launch into the day's lesson – The Psychology of Persuasion. It was supposed to be about consumer behavior, but somehow it always became about life. "Marketing," I said, "isn't about selling stuff. It's about storytelling – convincing people they need a $6 latte to feel alive."

A student in the front row raised her hand. "Is that gonna be on the test?"

"No," I sighed. "It's gonna be on your transcript."

The class blinked. I could almost hear their inner monologue: Is this guy okay?

Halfway through, I caught my reflection in the projector screen – older, grayer, and looking suspiciously like the ghost of Tenure Past. The new professors down the hall were busy installing TikTok on the syllabus, and here I was still grading with a red pen that leaked judgment.

But I still love it, in my own masochistic way. The chaos, the confusion, the kid who always asked if attendance counted. I especially love when, weeks later, a lightbulb flickered on in a student's head – sometimes faint, but still there.

At the end of class, I pack up my laptop (after a brief argument with the HDMI cable), and muttered my usual farewell: "Go make something matter. Or, at least something funny."

WHEN TECHNOLOGY TOOK A PERSONAL DAY

It was supposed to be an ordinary Tuesday at the university–Intro to Marketing, 8:00 a.m., Room 214. The syllabus called for a dazzling multimedia presentation on "The Digital Revolution in Branding." I had prepared a slideshow so good it could have sold snow to Canadians. Animated charts, embedded videos, even one of those smug little infographics that made me feel like a TED Talk star.

At 7:59 a.m., everything was perfect. By 8:00, everything had gone to hell.

The projector hummed, flickered, and then displayed what looked like the world's saddest shade of blue. The sound system began crackling like it was trying to summon Morse code for "abandon ship." And my laptop–the one I had just updated "for security reasons"–was now proudly refusing to connect to Wi-Fi.

I tried the standard academic IT incantation:"Control-Alt-Pray." Nothing.

"Okay," I said to the class, pacing in front of the dead projector, "let's pivot. This is a live demonstration of marketing's greatest lesson: improvisation."

From the back, a student murmured, "Is this on the exam?"

"It might be," I said, glaring, "if the exam works."

I grabbed a dry-erase marker, only to discover that every single one had died in solidarity with the technology. The whiteboard became a smear of gray sadness, like the aftermath of a toddler's art project.

So I did what professors of a certain vintage do best–I told stories. I went off-script. I became the analog hero of the digital apocalypse.

"Back before PowerPoint," I said, "we had something magical called eye contact. And when a student fell asleep, we knew it wasn't because of screen glare–it was pure boredom, the honest kind."

The students laughed–real laughter, not emoji laughter. Phones were down. Laptops were shut. They were… listening.

I explained branding by comparing it to relationships: "Marketing is just dating with spreadsheets. You tell someone what they want to hear, you promise consistency, and then they leave you for someone flashier."

By 9:20, they were hooked. They debated, argued, and one student even took notes by hand.

When the class ended, I looked at the blank projector, still glowing faintly like a remorseful ghost. I took a sip of my coffee—lukewarm, of course— and grinned.

"Technology," I said, "may enhance teaching, but it doesn't replace it. Especially when it's on strike."

That night, IT emailed to say everything was working again.

I didn't reply.

I was too busy ordering a fresh pack of markers—and quietly wondering if maybe, just maybe, I taught better when nothing worked at all.

THE LECTURE THAT WOULDN'T DIE

After thirty-some years of teaching, I had heard every excuse known to humankind—and possibly a few invented by extraterrestrials. My favorites were the classics: "My laptop crashed," "My dog ate my thumb drive," and the perennial "I didn't know we had homework." But modern times had ushered in new masterpieces of creativity: "ChatGPT forgot to save my essay," "I got shadow-banned from the learning portal," and the hauntingly sincere, "I had to attend my hamster's emotional support therapy."

I used to correct students gently. Now I just nod. "Sure. Hamster trauma. Valid reason."

Each semester, the course titles changed slightly—Digital Marketing Strategies became Strategic Digital Marketing—but the content stayed the same. I could deliver the lecture on Consumer Motivation in my sleep, and once, I was pretty sure I did.

I'd start with enthusiasm, gesturing toward the PowerPoint like a man

PREHISTORIC
PREDICTIVE
ANALYTICS

unveiling art. "Maslow's hierachy of needs! Every decision you make ties back to it!" But somewhere around slide twelve, I could feel my voice slipping into autopilot—an old vinyl record skipping on the same groove.

Even my jokes had tenure. The one about impulse buying toilet paper during a snowstorm still got polite chuckles, but I could see it in their faces: Grandpa's running the nostalgia reel again.

I began to notice the signs. I'd catch myself using phrases like, "Back when social media meant bulletin boards," or, "I remember when marketing had real jingles." The new assistant professors floated past in sneakers that cost more than my first car, buzzing about "brand ecosystems" and "engagement funnels."

One afternoon, after yet another lecture on consumer behavior that I'd given so many times it might qualify as a sacred ritual, I looked out over the sea of glowing laptop screens and thought, Maybe it's time.

Not out of bitterness—I still loved the spark when a student's idea clicked. But the fire that once burned like espresso now sputtered like decaf.

I leaned on the podium and smiled. "You know," I told my class, "marketing is just storytelling. You've got to know when to keep the story going—and when to end it before it loses the plot."

The students nodded, half-listening, half-doom-scrolling.

I smiled again, a private grin this time. I knew I wasn't done teaching—just maybe done grading. I dreamed there were other audiences out there. Smaller, more honest ones.

Perhaps a classroom with talking animals, mischievous fairies, and moral lessons disguised as giggles.

I sipped my coffee and made a mental note: Next semester, maybe the students will be five years old—and finally willing to listen.

THE MARCH OF MODERNITY

I prided himself on being adaptable. After all, I had survived the transition from chalkboards to smartboards, from memos to emails, and from "Please see attached" to "Oops, forgot the attachment." But lately, I'd begun to suspect the world had shifted into a gear I didn't have. Evolving is an important part of my DNA and leveling-up my tech creds could possibly help me to better understand my students.

It started with social media. Once, I thought "influencer" was a term for someone in a multilevel marketing scheme. Now, apparently, it was a legitimate profession. My students have "brands," "followings," and "content strategies." I have gout, a cat, and a Hotmail password I can't remember.

I tried to keep up. I joined LinkedIn, where strangers congratulated me for "work anniversaries" I didn't know I had. I downloaded TikTok to "study the culture," but all it did was convince that my attention span now had the half-life of a sneeze.

I once went the university's "Innovation Initiative." A twenty-something in designer sneakers was hired to "modernize the learning experience." He explained to me that lectures were "outdated" and that students preferred "immersive, gamified learning environments."

"So," I asked, "you want me to teach marketing through interpretive dance?"

The young man blinked. "That's… actually not a bad idea."

Determined to stay relevant, Maddog experimented with jargon. During one lecture he announced, "Today we'll ideate a synergistic branding paradigm." His students stared. One raised her hand. "Dr. M, are you okay?"

I wasn't sure.

Even my wardrobe came under attack. Princess Laura suggested I "refresh my look." The next week he showed up to campus in a hoodie that said

#MarketingLegend. The students assumed it was ironic and made it a meme. I was famous–for about four hours.

Still, I fought the good fight. I learned to screen share without accidentally showing my grocery list. I mastered the mute button (eventually). And when the administration replaced office hours with "virtual open-door sessions," I simply moved my laptop to the kitchen and brewed another pot of coffee.

But the moment that broke me came during a department meeting. A bright young assistant professor declared, "We're rebranding education for the digital native generation."

I leaned back in my chair. "I've been teaching since dial-up, kid. I'm not rebranding–I'm rebooting."

The room laughed. I smiled faintly, realizing I'd just become the department's living museum exhibit–– flip-phone and all.

Later that evening, I sat at my desk, staring at my reflection in the dark laptop screen. "Maybe," I said aloud, "relevance isn't about keeping up. Maybe it's about refusing to disappear."

I took a sip of coffee and smiled. "Besides, I'll go viral when they least expect it."

Then Daisy the cat stepped on the keyboard, accidentally sending a half-written syllabus to the entire faculty listserv.

Within the hour, the subject line–"WEEK ONE: PANIC"–had 74 likes and a meme.

I was trending. Finally.

THE DAILY ROUTINE OF THE UNRETIRED

I still arrived every morning at 7:45 a.m. sharp–because that was the magical moment when the faculty lounge coffee was "least poisoned by committee meetings" and "hadn't yet absorbed the despair of the day." By 7:50, I claimed, the pot tasted like warm cardboard and broken promises.

After securing my mug of survival juice, I wander the halls like an unofficial dean of morale, greeting new hires who routinely mistook me for some distinguished Emeritus legend.

"Good morning, sir," they'd say, standing a little straighter.

"Morning," I'd reply. "I taught your boss's boss. And your boss's boss's goldfish. Smart fish. Terrible note-taker."

I refused on principle to learn the new learning management system.

"I'm already managing my life, that's enough systems."

I wrote lectures by hand in a battered notebook and uploaded photos of the pages, calling it "vintage pedagogy." IT called it "a cry for help."

My laptop remained "the electric typewriter," a term that caused interns to spontaneously age five years. And I insisted I never made butt calls because I kept my flip-phone in my front pocket. "Physics and my fun-sized anatomy won't allow it," I'd say confidently.

Eventually, HR scheduled a "Retirement Consultation." I arrived wearing tweed, carrying a folder labeled REASONS TO KEEP ME, color-coded and tabbed. HR sent me home with pamphlets about hobbies and "active aging." I sent them back the next day–annotated.

"Golf: glorified wandering."

"Knitting: too stabby."

"Birdwatching: suspiciously slow."

"Pickleball: for people who fear tennis."

And so I remained–unretired, unbothered, and undefeated–showing up every morning with coffee, confidence, and an unshakable belief that I still had something to teach… even if the new hires thought I came with the building.

THE GREAT RETIREMENT REBELLION

My colleagues had begun whispering that it was time. Not an intervention exactly—more of a gentle nudge toward the sunset.

I'd been at the university since the Nixon administration, had taught three generations of the same family, and owned more expired ID badges than the campus security office. My office looked less like a workplace and more like a historical exhibit: a museum of coffee rings, yellowed memos, and long-dead markers.

But retire?

Not a chance.

"They can take my parking pass," I declared, "when they pry it from my cold, coffee-stained fingers."

The dean tried subtle hints. "Dr. Mark, have you ever considered... slowing down?"

"Slowing down?" I barked. "That's how people die in nature documentaries!"

Next came the Retirement Seminar, which I attended only to heckle. The presenter spoke gently about "finding new purpose." I raised my hand and asked if the new purpose could involve staying on payroll.

They offered me a gold watch. I countered with a request for a gold espresso machine. Negotiations stalled.

My students love me, though most assumed I'd been tenured sometime during the Industrial Revolution. "Professor Maddog's been here forever," one whispered. "I think he invented the syllabus."

I started using their misconceptions to my advantage.

"Yes," I told a freshman, "I was there when marketing began. We had apples when they were still a fruit, used stone tablets, and off-the-rack emotional manipulation."

FACULTY
RETIREMENT
SEMINAR

Humpty Was Gently Pushed

Finally, the Dean cornered him one afternoon. "Mark," she said gently, "don't you want to enjoy retirement?"

"Oh, I do," I replied. "I'm just not ready to start it."

She sighed. "You can't keep teaching forever."

I smiled. "Maybe not. But I can keep mentoring the ones who think they invented creativity."

And with that, he strutted down the hall, coffee mug in hand, as though the corridor itself played his theme music—something between a jazz riff and a caffeine overdose.

Because retirement, to Dr. Maddog, wasn't a finish line. It was a marketing concept he refused to buy.

After all, I liked my brand just the way it was:

A little eccentric, a little outdated, and still trending in wisdom.

It began innocently enough—or so I thought. A few polite comments from colleagues, the kind that sound complimentary until you translate them.

"You've had such a long and distinguished career," they said, with that careful tone usually reserved for obituaries and antique clocks.

Or: "Your teaching style is so… classic."

Or the dead giveaway: "Have you ever thought about how much free time you'd have if you retired?"

I knew what was happening. I'd seen the signs before—in department meetings where the younger faculty spoke in acronyms he didn't recognize, in memos that started with "As we modernize our curriculum," and in the way they always gave me the seat farthest from the projector, as if protecting me from technology.

I naturally brought the problem to the Coffee Club.

Ralph, ever sympathetic, said, "Retirement's not the end—it's just an extended coffee break."

Daisy suggested, "You could teach workshops on something you love—like sweater collecting."

Hugh, the dreamer, offered, "Or you could finally write that memoir: The Professor Who Refused to Log Out."

I sipped my coffee and considered. Maybe they were right. Maybe it wasn't the end of something, but the beginning of my next chapter—the one where he didn't have to grade papers written entirely by AI, or learn what "learning outcomes alignment metrics" meant.

I imagined mornings without meetings, afternoons wandering thrift stores, evenings writing children's books with Daisy the cat supervising from the keyboard. I could still teach, just not to a classroom—maybe to the world, one curious mind at a time.

So at the next faculty meeting, when the dean cleared his throat and said, "Dr. Mark, have you thought about your future plans?" I smiled serenely and replied, "Yes. I plan to have one."

There was silence. Then polite applause. Then relief—mostly theirs.

I walked out into the hallway, free, humming softly to himself. I wasn't retiring. I was rebranding—from Professor Emeritus to Adventurer-in-Residence.

And as I told the Coffee Club later, "They didn't nudge me out. They just reminded me where the door was—and I decided to hold it open for myself."

Dr. Maddog and the Silicon Circus

When I retired from academia, I didn't really retire. Like most professors, I simply switched offices, swapped jargon, and found a new audience to lecture–this time, they called it "consulting."

The idea seemed brilliant at first. After all, I had decades of wisdom, a bookshelf full of framed diplomas, and an entire library of PowerPoint slides polished through the Clinton, Bush, Obama, and caffeine administrations. Surely, the corporate world would bow before the mighty intellect of Dr. Maddog.

When I finally decided to "dip a toe" into the world of corporate consulting, I didn't realize the pool was full of sharks wearing Patagonia vests.

After decades of teaching marketing to undergrads who thought "brand loyalty" meant sticking with the same energy drink through finals week, I figured consulting would be easy. "How hard can it be?" I told Princess Laura. "It's just teaching, but with better coffee and worse manners."

My first gig was with a high-powered tech firm whose mission statement read like a ransom note. They were "leveraging synergies to reimagine scalable solutions across the digital ecosystem." I spent the first week trying to figure out if that meant they sold apps or anxiety.

The office looked like a spaceship designed by minimalists: glass walls, beanbag chairs, and a meditation pod that looked suspiciously like a broom closet with Wi-Fi. The dress code was "business casual futurist," which meant sneakers that cost more than his mortgage and blazers that had never seen a wrinkle–or a reason to exist.

I showed up in a tweed jacket, carrying a leather notebook and a coffee thermos that smelled faintly of tenure. The receptionist scanned me like a barcode. "You must be… external talent?"

I smiled. "External, yes. Talent… negotiable."

By noon, I was in a meeting called a "branding alignment huddle," which was neither aligned nor huddled. A young VP named Skyler (because of

SYNERDEATION INC.

course he was named Skyler) explained the goal: "We're not selling products—we're selling purpose."

"Ah," I said, "so… not money?"

Skyler laughed like a man who'd never seen a paycheck with deductions. "We're optimizing brand authenticity. We're building emotional ecosystems."

I scribbled in my notebook: Translate into English later.

After three hours of buzzwords, I'd had enough. "Look," I said, leaning back, "marketing is simple. Find out what people want, make it, and tell them why they need it before they realize they don't."

The room fell silent. Someone blinked. Someone else slowly sipped a kale smoothie. Skyler cleared his throat. "That's… not exactly how we frame it."

"I imagine not," I said. "But it works."

Despite my heresy, the firm kept inviting me back. Partly because my ideas worked, and partly because they found me fascinating—like a wise old monk who occasionally swore. When the interns discovered I didn't have WhatsAp, they reacted as though I'd confessed to carving messages in stone tablets.

I endured meetings where "ideation sessions" replaced thinking, and PowerPoint decks stretched longer than most relationships. But occasionally, amid the nonsense, I found a spark of brilliance—a reminder that human creativity still existed, buried beneath jargon and jugs of Kombucha.

By month three, the CEO asked him what he thought of their new campaign slogan: "Tomorrow Begins Today."

I looked at it and said, "That's not a slogan—that's a time paradox."

They printed it anyway.

THE REVENGE OF THE GRAYBEARD

It began, as these things often do, with an innocent meeting and a bad cup of coffee.

I sat in the conference room surrounded by a herd of freshly minted MBAs—young, confident, and collectively armed with enough jargon to choke a thesaurus. They spoke in acronyms and PowerPoint slides, using "synergy" like it was punctuation.

I'd been invited as "an experienced perspective," which, translated from corporate-speak, meant the old guy who remembers when ideas were written on paper instead of post-it walls shaped like unicorns.

It was going well until I suggested something sensible—like patience, or thought—and one of the interns, barely old enough to rent a car, smirked and said, "Okay, Boomer."

The room chuckled. I did not. My eyebrow twitched—a dangerous sign. The Graybeard had been awakened.

That night, over a restorative pot of coffee and a heated conversation with Daisy the cat ("They mock wisdom, Daisy! They mock experience!"), I devised my plan. It was elegant. It was diabolical. It involved spreadsheets, Latin, and office supplies.

Phase One: The Email Gambit

At precisely 6:04 a.m., I began firing off emails filled with historical references, mixed metaphors, and questions like, "Did you back up the cloud to the other cloud?" By the time the MBAs rolled in with their cold brews and wireless earbuds, their inboxes had become philosophical mazes.

"Why does he sign everything 'Yours in Perpetuity'?" one whispered.

"He sent me a spreadsheet in Lotus format," said another. "What's Lotus?"

Phase Two: The Meeting from the Depths

I scheduled a "Strategic Vision Alignment Roundtable." No one knew what it meant, but attendance was mandatory. When the MBAs arrived, he handed out printed agendas—on paper—and asked everyone to write their ideas by hand.

Confusion spread like wildfire. "Can we open a shared doc?" someone asked.

"No," I said. "We'll be using shared pens."

I then delivered a 45-minute PowerPoint that contained only one slide: a black screen with white text reading, "Wisdom uploads slowly."

Halfway through, he paused dramatically, stared at the ceiling, and muttered, "Back in my day, we didn't have analytics dashboards. We had intuition, and it worked 60% of the time, every time."

Phase Three: The Digital Reckoning

Knowing my adversaries lived by apps, I began subtly sabotaging their tech ecosystem. One morning, I replaced the office Wi-Fi password with "dialupnoise1987." The next, I set their Slack notification sound to a dial tone.

By the end of the week, the MBAs were twitching, unshaven, and mumbling things like "He sent me a fax. How do I reply to a fax?"

When the boss finally intervened, I simply smiled and said, "Just trying to bridge the generation gap. Some of us use bridges; others use buzzwords."

The MBAs, humbled and exhausted, offered me a truce. They even stopped saying "Okay Boomer." (At least within earshot.)

When I returned home, I leaned back in my chair, sipped my coffee, and whispered to Daisy, "They think the war is over. But next week... I'm introducing them to the overhead projector."

And somewhere deep in the Wi-Fi router, a fax machine beeped in approval.

Eventually, I left the firm on good terms (they gave me a hoodie with the company logo, which I now uses as a rag for polishing my car).

As I walked out of their gleaming glass building for the last time, I shook my head and smiled. "Consulting," I muttered. "It's like academia—but

Wisdom
uploads
slowly.

with more meetings and fewer books."

Then I took a deep breath, looked up at the sky, and thought, Maybe I'll go back to teaching. At least the freshmen admit they're confused.

With quitting not a part of my DNA, I took a second gig with firm that described itself as being "on the bleeding edge of disruption." That phrase alone should have been a warning. By the end of my first meeting, I realized "disruption" was just a fancy word for chaos with snacks.

"Let's keep this agile," one executive said. "We'll circle back, loop in marketing, and synergize across verticals."

I blinked. "Is that English or interpretive dance?"

I spent the first month trying to decode this companies language. Meetings weren't meetings–they were "strategy syncs." Brainstorms were "ideation sprints." Nobody had ideas anymore; they ideated.

When I proudly handed out a 20-page report with charts and references, the team leader glanced at it and asked, "Can you turn this into a one-slide summary for the deck?"

I took a deep breath. "The deck? You mean the thing with 300 bullet points that nobody reads?"

"Exactly!"

The shift from academia to consulting was becoming like going from writing Shakespeare to ghostwriting fortune cookies. In the classroom, my students feigned interest but at least pretended to take notes. In the boardroom, executives nodded enthusiastically while secretly checking their stock portfolios.

I quickly learned that in corporate life, the truth mattered less than the optics. "Perception is reality," they told me. "Data is just a story with confidence issues."

During one engagement, I proposed a thoughtful, evidence-based marketing strategy. The VP of Brand smiled and said, "Love it, but can we make it go viral?"

I sipped my coffee and muttered, "If I knew how to do that, I'd be on a beach somewhere, not explaining consumer psychology to you people."

Still, there were moments of triumph. Once, during a particularly tedious Zoom call, I asked the team to "stop pretending to innovate and start trying to be useful." The stunned silence was followed by slow, reluctant applause.

By the end of his first year, I had mastered the corporate art of looking productive: walking fast with a coffee cup, saying "great question" when I had no idea what was asked, and using "let's unpack that" as a stall tactic.

But deep down, I missed the messiness of teaching—the dry eraser pen stained cuffs, the blank stares, the half-baked ideas that occasionally bloomed into brilliance.

Consulting paid better, sure. But it was missing something vital: the joyful chaos of students learning to think.

One night, as I sat alone revising a slide deck titled "Optimizing Brand Synergy in the Post-Digital Paradigm", I chuckled to myself.

I closed my laptop, poured a drink, and said aloud, "I've officially become what I used to make fun of."

Then I raised my glass and toasted the empty room.

"To synergy," I said. "And the billable hour."

YOUNG
FOSSIL

SEVENTY AND STILL IDLING LOUDLY

I sat at the kitchen table one morning, staring into my coffee like it might hold the answer to life's most pressing question: What exactly is a seventy-year-old supposed to do when he's not dead yet?

I was, by all accounts, supposed to be "slowing down." The problem was—I didn't feel slow. My knees creaked like old floorboards, sure, and my back sometimes composed its own protest symphony when he bent over too fast, but the mind? Still running laps around most of the world.

"I'm not done," I muttered into my mug. Daisy the cat, unimpressed as always, flicked her tail in agreement or disdain—hard to tell which.

The world, it seemed, had other opinions. Former colleagues had started using that awful tone people reserve for grandparents and malfunctioning computers. "How are you, Dr. Maddog?" they'd say slowly, like he might not remember. "Keeping busy?"

Keeping busy? I had a to-do list longer than a CVS receipt. I was halfway through three books, advising two nonprofits, and still trying to figure out why my coffeemaker made that wheezing noise every morning.

"I've got plenty of gas left in the tank," I said, standing up and immediately sitting back down because my left hip disagreed. "Fine—premium fuel, questionable suspension."

The trouble was that retirement, in theory, sounded delightful—travel, naps, no meetings—but in practice, it was like being sent to the penalty box of life. I missed the chaos of classrooms, the whiteboard arguments, the coffee-fueled brainstorming that stretched past common sense.

Now people expected me to garden. To putter. I don't putter. I scheme. I plan. I brew metaphors like coffee—strong and overcomplicated.

"I'm seventy, not obsolete," I told Princess Laura over breakfast.

She looked up from her lesson plans. "You said that yesterday."

"Well, it's still true today."

What really gnawed at me wasn't the number—it was the assumption that it meant something final. Seventy wasn't an ending; it was just Act Three, with better jokes and lower metabolism.

I still had ideas—too many, in fact. A few were ridiculous, but that had never stopped me before. There was a children's book about a philosophical squirrel, a half-written essay on how academia should teach empathy instead of metrics, and a personal goal to make Daisy Instagram famous (though the cat refused all modeling contracts).

I sipped my coffee, stretched, and smirked. "Plenty of gas left in the tank," I said again, louder this time. "Might need a tune-up, but I'm not parking yet."

I stood, grabbed my notebook, and started scribbling furiously. The cat watched, unimpressed but curious, as the man who refused to retire plotted his next great adventure.

Because for me, seventy wasn't an age. It was an engine—still running, slightly louder, and very much alive.

Old Age—The Longest Practical Joke

Everyone says aging is a gift. I disagree. I'm convinced old age is more like a practical joke designed by the universe, complete with creaky knees, leaky bladders, and an endless supply of mailers reminding you that you now qualify for "senior savings."

Let's start with the good news: getting old isn't all bad. I finally get to say things like "back in my day" and "they don't make 'em like they used to"—even if you're just talking about Pop-Tarts. I've develop an uncanny ability to predict the weather with my joints, and strangers have started calling me "sir" without even being sarcastic.

With age comes wisdom—or at least the ability to remember things that happened before Google existed. After six decades of trial and error, I finally know which brand of duct tape actually fixes things, which grocery line is the slowest (all of them), and how to fake sleep during family political debates. That's called experience, and it's priceless.

Then there are the discounts. Suddenly, I'm a member of every senior savings program in a hundred-mile radius. I get ten percent off my pancakes, my coffee, and my movie ticket—if I can stay awake through the movie. And let's not forget fashion freedom. I've earned the right to wear whatever I please. Hawaiian shirts, socks with sandals, pajama pants at the grocery store—it's not poor taste, it's confidence. People call it "eccentric," which is just society's polite way of saying, "You've stopped caring what we think."

Selective hearing becomes another gift of age. I can conveniently tune out anything unpleasant—tax advice, political arguments, or anyone saying "Let's do a group text!" Yet somehow, I can still hear the cookie jar open from across the house. And naps? Naps are now a respected lifestyle. You can fall asleep mid-conversation, mid-sandwich, or mid-episode of Jeopardy! and nobody bats an eye. They just drape a blanket over you and whisper, "He's earned it."

Of course, it's not all victory laps and afternoon snoozes. Gravity, for one, becomes your sworn enemy. Everything on your body starts migrating

south–your arms, your face, even your enthusiasm. Getting out of bed each morning turns into a two-act performance: Act One is stretching, groaning, and muttering; Act Two is the grand finale, where you actually stand up.

Another cruelty of old age is that technology evolves while I devolve. Smartphones, streaming services, apps–each one an opportunity to feel stupid.

I once tried to text "OK" but accidentally ordered a kayak online. Another time, I yelled at Siri to "turn off the lights" and instead ordered a pizza in Ohio. "Old age means being outsmarted daily by a rectangle in your pocket."

Then comes the mirror. Once, I looked into it and saw youth: bright eyes, thick hair, a smile. Now? My reflection looks like I've been in the pool way too long..

The hair has retreated, the wrinkles have advanced, and nose hairs grow like they're competing in a county fair vegetable contest. Every morning is a new surprise: a liver spot here, a wrinkle there, a rogue eyebrow hair pointing true north.

Forgetfulness comes free with senior discounts. I walk into a room and instantly forget why. I put glasses on my head, then search the house for an hour. I once introduced Daisy the Cat to guests as "our nephew, Daniel."

Sure, forgetting makes life harder. But it also makes life… repetitive. I get to enjoy reruns of my own stories. "The kids laugh every time, mostly because they've heard it twelve times."

Even my car keys have developed a mischievous streak, hiding themselves in places I'd swear I'd already checked.

Then there are the aches and pains. Once upon a time, I hurt because I did something exciting–skiing, hiking, dancing. Now I hurt because I slept weird.

"Did I run a marathon last night? Did I wrestle a bear? No. I just… slept."

Every joint now sounds like bubble wrap, and by the time I reach the toilet, I'm already winded. Nothing proves old age sucks more than the bladder. It doesn't obey normal rules anymore. It calls the shots. It wakes me up three times a night with an urgent summons, only to deliver a trickle. And somewhere along the way my regular tip was replaced with a sprinkler head.

During the day, my bladder keeps time like a metronome: coffee, toilet, water, toilet, sneeze, toilet.

And perhaps the most noticeable change: the filter between your brain and your mouth starts to thin. You say exactly what you're thinking, and it feels great—until your family reminds you that telling the waitress, "I used to have a figure like yours before gravity got me," isn't technically a compliment.

Getting older also means more doctors than friends. Every week it's another appointment: cardiologist, urologist, dermatologist, podiatrist. He once told Princess Laura that the only "ologist' that I don't have is a paleontologist, and that's just because I avoid museums.

Each doctor says the same thing: eat healthier, walk more, cut out bacon. I smile, nod, and ignores them. "If old age already sucks why make it worse by eating kale? And no bacon, WTF!"

In the end, getting old is a bit like owning an antique car. You creak, you leak, and you require frequent maintenance—but when you're polished up and running, people still stop to admire you. You've earned the right to complain about the weather, forget your passwords, and fall asleep at 8 p.m.

YANKEES
NY

THE NOBLE ART OF THE AFTERNOON NAP

There comes a point every day – usually around the same time the afternoon sunlight starts judging me through the blinds – when I declars, "I am not tired… I am simply reallocating energy."

This, of course, is code for nap time.

I approach the event with ceremony. The couch is fluffed. The cat, Daisy, is negotiated with. ("You take the left cushion, I'll take the right. No claws, no politics.") A throw blanket is summoned – the faded tartan one from Salvation Army. Before lying down, I always check the time, not because it matters but so I can later say, "I only closed my eyes for fifteen minutes," when it was, in fact, a full REM cycle and two snack breaks later.

I arrange myself like a man about to undergo spiritual levitation. One leg bent, one arm over my head, mouth slightly open in case inspiration or a passing gnat wanders in. My last thought before drifting off is usually something profound, like, "I should probably move that laundry… tomorrow."

THEN – BLISS.

The nap itself is not quiet. There's snoring, sighing, mumbling, and once a full debate with myself about whether soup counts as a beverage. Daisy occasionally joins the chorus, adding purrs and the occasional judgmental stare.

To outsiders, this may look like sleep. To me, it is maintenance mode. The mind defrags. The body reboots. The soul briefly visits a place where there are no bills, deadlines, or lower back pain.

But awakening – that's where the real drama begins.

I always wake up startled, as if I've been teleported to a parallel universe where time has advanced by four hours and all my good intentions expired. My hair looks like it's been styled by a leaf blower and a balloon. My shirt bears mysterious creases in the shape of a remote control.

"Where am I?" I mumble, staggering upright. "Did I time travel? Did I miss lunch?"

I check my phone. Six missed calls, three texts, and one calendar reminder reading, "You said you'd get stuff done."

I nods solemnly. "Yes. I did say that. Past me was a bit of an optimist."

And yet – as the fog clears, there's that undeniable sense of triumph. The nap has worked its magic. The world feels slightly softer. The brain hums like a machine that's just been oiled in espresso.

I stretch, yawn, and announce to the empty room, "I have successfully completed my daily system reboot. Let productivity recommence!"

I then make a beeline for the coffee pot.

Because nothing complements a good nap like the taste of another bad idea.

Because let's be honest: getting old sure beats the alternative.

THE ANNUAL INSPECTION

Being chronologically gifted I approach the doctor's office the way one might approach a suspicious-looking buffet–curious, hungry for answers, but fully aware something unsettlingly worse than gas station sushi might be lurking under the lid.

I put this visit off for months. Maybe years. I wasn't sure; time, like my waistline, had gotten a little stretchy. But recently, my body had begun sending me strongly worded memos. My knees crackled like campfires, my back filed formal complaints, and my bladder had adopted an internship schedule–reporting for duty every two hours, day and night.

As I sat in the waiting room, I flipped through a magazine from the Paleozoic era titled "Men's Health: January 2014 Edition." The cover model looked like he'd never eaten a carbohydrate or made a bad life choice. I scowled and muttered, "Amateur."

The nurse called my name–cheerful, efficient, and terrifying. She weighed me, measured me, and took my blood pressure, which–judging by her raised eyebrow–was either impressive or evidence that his arteries were trying to secede.

"Have you been exercising?" she asked.

"Of course," I said proudly. "I get plenty of steps looking for my glasses every morning."

She made a note, the kind of note nurses make when they've heard that joke a hundred times but are too polite to call you on it.

Then came the doctor–young, unnervingly upbeat, and looking like Doogie Howser. "Well, Dr. Maddog," he began, scanning the chart, "how are we feeling today?"

"Oh, mostly vertical," I replied. "A few parts are squeaking, and I've started making sound effects when I sit down. That's new."

The doctor chuckled in the way that doctors do right before prescribing kale. "That's perfectly normal for someone your age."

Of course I bristled. "You say that like I'm an endangered species."

"Not at all," said the doctor. "Just part of getting older."

"'Getting older' is something that happens to other people," I protested. "I was planning to skip that phase entirely. I'm going to live to be 140, so what you are currently admiring is my mid-life crisis. I even own a red Porsche to prove it. "

The doctor nodded sympathetically and began the ritual poking, prodding, and shining lights into orifices that had never requested illumination. "Any concerns?" he asked.

"Well," I said, counting on his fingers, "I creak when I bend, wheeze when I climb stairs, and occasionally forget why I walked into a room. Also, I've developed a relationship with my heating pad that may not be entirely appropriate."

The doctor laughed, then offered advice that could have been printed on a bumper sticker: "Eat better. Move more. Sleep enough. Kale."

"Excellent," I said. "So basically, do the opposite of everything that makes life enjoyable."

I left the office with a clean bill of health and a pamphlet titled 'Healthy Aging: How to Pretend You're Fine.' Outside, I took a deep breath of fresh air, stretched my back until something audibly popped, and smiled.

I might be creaky, leaky, and slightly forgetful—but by God, he was still Dr. Maddog, patron saint of coffee, chaos, and survival.

And tomorrow morning, I will celebrate my vitality the only way I know how: by pouring an extra-large mug of Joe and raising it with my Pee O'Clock to the noble art of staying upright.

THE GREAT LITERARY LEAP

After four decades of lecturing about marketing, mentoring clueless interns, and surviving one too many "strategic realignments," I had an epiphany one Tuesday morning somewhere between my second cup of coffee and my third complaint about autocorrect.

I didn't want to consult anymore.

I didn't want to teach another PowerPoint full of buzzwords about "emotional engagement" and "brand storytelling."

I wanted to tell my own stories.

"I'm going to write children's books," I announced to Princess Laura.

She didn't even look up from her lesson plan. "Good. Start with the one about the old man who refuses to retire."

And so began the next great chapter of my life–literally.

At first, I thought it would be easy. How hard could it be? I'd read to enough nieces, nephews and grand-puppies to know the basic formula: cute animal + moral lesson + light rhyming = bestseller.

I bought a notebook, sharpened a pencil, and wrote:

Once upon a time, there was a very tired professor…

Then I stared at it for three hours.

Apparently, the hard part wasn't the writing. It was the unlearning. In academia, you're rewarded for being complicated. In children's literature, you get thrown out for using the word "synergize."

When I presented my first draft, "The Marketing Squirrel and the Five Ps of the Forest," my test audience (three preschoolers and one mildly interested cat) gave it two yawns and a juice box to the floor.

Undeterred, I pivoted to whimsy. A Dancing Dandelion, The Boy Who Taped Leaves back on trees, and the instant classic, Rocky, a rescue dog that got fat because he liked his name.

I discovered that writing for children was like teaching marketing to adults: they both need to be tricked into learning something. The only difference was that kids were more honest. When a line didn't land, they didn't fake laugh. They just asked, "Why?"—which was both humbling and infuriating.

I also learned that "writing children's books" doesn't mean "shorter hours." My mornings became coffee-fueled marathons of rhyming couplets and plot holes the size of Lake Erie. I argued with myself about whether a talking teacup should have feelings and if a buffalo could wear gym shorts ethically.

Still, there was something magical about it. For the first time in decades, I wasn't trying to sell or persuade. I was creating worlds. I was making mischief. I was laughing—really laughing—at my own work.

When I brought my first finished manuscript to a local library for story hour, I was terrified. But as I read aloud—my voice full of silly enthusiasm—something unexpected happened: the kids listened. They laughed. They gasped. One little girl shouted, "Read it again!"

And just like that, I knew I'd found his next great lecture hall.

No projectors. No jargon. No performance reviews.

Just imagination, laughter, and the occasional spilled juice box.

That night, as I sat at my desk surrounded by crumpled drafts, I smiled and whispered, "I guess I'm still teaching—just smaller humans with better attention spans."

Then I raised my mug of coffee in a toast to the blank page.

"To my new students," I said, "and to finally having a syllabus worth following."

Now, I know what you're thinking. Children's books? Is that a job?

I've asked myself the same question. It doesn't look like work. But behind the whimsy, there's the grind: counting syllables, balancing stanzas, chiseling away at a story until it sings.

Of course, my family doesn't buy this. My wife calls it "retirement with crayons." My kids tell their friends, "Yeah, our dad argues with a spider all night and writes about fairies all day." My 95-year old mom just shakes her head and plops down to whip online strangers' butts at Words With Friends.

But to me, this is work. Real work. Harder than anyone thinks. Writing for children means distilling the whole complicated mess of life into something simple enough for a bedtime story. That's not easy. That's alchemy.

And so I clock in, mug in hand, bare feet, staring at a blank page that's somehow louder than Daisy's claws scratching at the bathroom door at 3 a.m.

Living The Dream

I realize I've become the literary equivalent of a crockpot: still on, just set to low. Semi-retired, they call it. Not retired. Semi, like a truck that still barrels down the highway, only with more bathroom breaks and a better playlist.

The mirror in the hallway caught me passing and said, "Dr. Maddog, you used to be a newspaper publisher, an advertising-and-marketing guru, and a university professor. What are you now?"

"A children's book author," I replied, fluffing what little remains of my hair."

The mirror smirked. "That explains the glitter in your eyebrows."

It's true. You can measure my career path in adhesives: hot wax from page dummies, spray mount from ad comps, and now an industrial snowfall of craft-glitter that will outlive the glaciers.

Datelines, Deadlines, and Bedtimes

As a newspaper publisher, I lived by the doctrine of ink and panic. Mornings smelled like newsprint and coffee strong enough to christen a ship. We measured time in editions and adrenaline. "Stop the presses!" was less a command and more a hobby. My wardrobe was "stain-forward." My vocabulary: lede, nut graf, heds, decks, and "who left their lunch in the darkroom again."

Back then, I wrote headlines like carving jack-o-lanterns: quick, sharp, and likely to startle the neighbors. The paper taught me how to cut words until they squealed, and to get scoops without getting sued. We chased stories at midnight and stapled the morning to doorsteps by sunrise.

Now my deadlines involve bedtimes, and the only thing I chase at midnight is a runaway rhyme about Theresa's lost sock. I still write headlines, they're just longer: The Encyclopedia of Misunderstood Imaginary Monsters, and But I don't want to be a butterfly.

The The old newsroom instinct still kicks in. When a four-year-old raises a hand during story time and says, "That dragon's tax situation seems complicated," I can file a response under pressure. Also, I still fact-check: and yes, buffalo do not live downtown, they merely visit.

From Slogans to Soggy Cornflakes

Before newspapers, I wandered into advertising and marketing agencies where deadlines wear cologne. I learned to swim in a sea of acronyms: KPI, CPM, ROI, DIY (okay, that last one was just my weekend). I wrote taglines so sticky they could hold up your kid's science project.

That life prepared me perfectly for children's books. Every toddler is a focus group with jam on its face. Every parent is a brand manager with a bedtime budget. And a picture book? Thirty-two pages of pure campaign–launch day every day, my friend.

Lecture Pits, Story Hours

Woven in-between was the university. I taught bright minds and a few thoroughly napping ones. Office hours were a ritual where no one showed up until ten minutes before grades were due. I herded committees like fainting goats. I wrote syllabi so detailed they included contingency plans for meteor showers and printer jams. The motto was publish or perish. I chose publish and live with interesting nouns.

Teaching made me suspiciously good at presenting the same material seventeen ways while pretending it's brand new, which is basically what happens when you read your book to three first-grade classes in a row. Friends say I still walk into rooms like I'm about to give a lecture on "Applied Curiosity 401." They're not wrong. I do take attendance at the dinner table.

The Crew Rebrands Me (Again)

One morning on the porch, I informed the Coffee Council that I was officially semi-retired.

"From what?" Ralph asked. "You've had more careers than ketchup has uses."

"Publisher, marketer, professor," I said. "Now I make rhymes and manage glitter migration."

Daisy slid a plate of pastries between us like a treaty. "We're happy for you," she said. "But you're not the retiring type. You're… refiring."

My lecture voice now reads aloud, my ad brain writes jacket copy, and my publishing spine keeps the whole circus on schedule. Everything I used to do, only with more animals wearing hats.

Readings, Reactions, and ROI

(Return on Imagination)

At a recent library reading, I watched a boy in the front row mouth every word I read like he was catching fireflies. When I finished, he whispered, "Again." Not "more data," not "synergy," not "please address the rubric on page six." Just "Again."

In marketing meetings, I used to chase the mystical "engagement." At story time, engagement is when a girl in a unicorn hoodie leans forward so far she nearly becomes a bookmark. ROI? It's the parent who emails later: "He slept with the book under his pillow." That'll beat a click-through rate every day of the week.

Work from Home – It'll Be Peaceful

There was a time when "working from home" sounded like the ultimate reward for decades of labor – a retirement perk before retirement. I pictured myself in pajama pants, sipping artisanal coffee, tapping out genius ideas on my laptop while birds chirped and the cat purred in the background.

That was before I actually tried it.

Now, "remote work" feels more like an Olympic event that combines dodgeball, improv theater, and pest control. The first obstacle: distractions.

At precisely the moment I hit my creative stride, Daisy the cat decides to leap onto my keyboard to contribute 47 rows of "zzzzzzzzzzzz." The refrigerator hums judgmentally behind me – a constant siren song calling me toward leftover lasagna. Meanwhile, the coffee pot sputters like a coughing dragon, reminding me it's time for another refill (my sixth of the morning).

The Pee O'Clock Coffee Club doesn't help either. They show up – virtually, thank goodness – right when I should be writing. Running Ralph starts bragging about his new sneakers, and Deaf Hugh loudly hums Beethoven.

And every tech tool designed to "increase productivity" seems to have been engineered by Satan himself. My laptop freezes mid-sentence, Zoom mutes itself mysteriously, and PowerPoint crashes with the confidence of a kamikaze pilot.

By noon, I've written exactly one usable sentence: "As I was saying before the cat deleted my paragraph…"

By three o'clock, I've accepted my fate. I'm not working from home – I'm wandering from kitchen to coffee pot, occasionally sitting near a computer to make it look legitimate. After all, when your cat, your mom, and your coffee maker are your coworkers, every day is a sitcom waiting to be written.

WORKING IN THE CLOUDS

Eventually, I gave myself a promotion. I rented a real office on the 29th floor of a downtown office building.

There's something magical about the elevator ride, the security badge, the polite nods from nerd coders who assume I'm important because I'm old. They don't know that instead of JavaScript or Phase II funding, I spend my daydreams wondering whether a talking snowman would wear mittens.

From my window, the whole city stretches out. The lake glimmers like tin foil under the sun. The tiny cars inch along the Skyway like ants with deadlines. On a clear day, I can even imagine seeing the faint mist of Niagara Falls.

Other tenants are lawyers, consultants, and accountants. They speak in acronyms and bill by the quarter-hour. I sit at my desk with a notebook full of doodles, daydreaming about whether rabbits should pay bus fare. But from up here, daydreaming looks like productivity. Admiring the view counts as research. Procrastination is reframed as "scene-setting."

One neighbor once asked what I did. I smiled and said, "Creative sector." That seemed to satisfy him.

I should feel like an imposter. Instead, I feel legitimate. Like I finally have a real job, even if my job is daydreaming on company letterhead.

THE DAYDREAMER-IN-RESIDENCE

Writing children's books from the 29th floor is equal parts absurd and beautiful.

I stare out at the skyline, and my mind drifts. Pigeons become plot points. Passing clouds are metaphors. The sparkle of the lake is an enchanted kingdom. What looks like blank staring is work if you squint.

Blur the line just right, and idleness becomes industry. Admiring the horizon becomes "research." Doodling becomes drafting. And somewhere between the third cup of coffee and the fourth daydream, a story begins to take shape.

Do I sometimes nap in the chair? Hell yes. Do I sometimes leave with nothing written but pages of scribbles about talking vegetables? Absolutely. But in the strange math of the creative life, it counts.

The truth is, the office gives me dignity. It tells me, in its quiet, elevated way: your daydreams matter. Even if they're about snowmen, rabbits, and a fairy with questionable bladder control.

And so, every day, I ride the elevator down, walk to my car, and head home. I leave behind the wannabe entrepreneurs, the nerdy coders, the acronyms. I take with me only my notebooks, my doodles, and the sense that, in some small way, I've done a day's work.

If you call writing children's books a real job.

The Author Emerges

It was a literary Epiphany. The Tooth Fairy collects molars. The Sandman sprinkles sleep. The Easter Bunny hides eggs. But the Tinkle Fairy? She teaches little boys how to aim.

It started as a joke at Pee O'Clock. I was half-asleep, standing in the dark, and muttered, "What this world really needs is a fairy with better bathroom training skills." She's here to say, firmly and kindly: "Keep your eye on the prize, kiddo. The toilet bowl isn't a suggestion – it's the goal."

The more I thought about it, the more I realized this fairy filled a serious gap in the pantheon of childhood helpers. Parents whisper about it, teachers dread it, janitors live in fear of it: little boys, armed with small bladders and poor accuracy. Floors, walls, and innocent shoes everywhere suffer. Somebody had to step in.

Enter the Tinkle Fairy

In my draft sketches, she hovers above the porcelain battlefield like a coach at halftime. She doesn't scold. She encourages: "Ready… steady… aim! And remember, gravity is your teammate." The kitchen crew had mixed reviews.

Ralph thought it was genius. "No drips, no drops, just hit the spot!"

Daisy rolled her eyes and promptly insisted on modeling for the fairy.

Deaf Hugh stirred dramatically, claiming it was the "most noble cause since the invention of indoor plumbing."

When I told Princess Laura, she blinked once, twice, then said, "Well… if anyone can make it charming, it's you. I love the idea. I'm just not sure I'm the right person to proofread the bathroom rhymes."

And so, The Tinkle Fairy's Guide to Ready-Aim–Fire gained its most important chapter: teaching little boys how to drown the Cheerios™. Funny, yes. Practical, absolutely. Maybe even world-saving, depending on the janitor. Because sometimes the difference between chaos and civilization is just one magical fairy saying, "Eyes forward, hands steady, and for heaven's sake – flush."

The Tinkle Fairy Arrives

Every writer eventually dreams of their magnum opus – that one defining work that cements their name in literary history. For Hemingway, it was *The Old Man and the Sea.* For Tolstoy, *War and Peace.* For me? *It's The Tinkle Fairy's Guide to Ready–Aim–Fire.*

After years of bladder-driven research, it only made sense to turn my midnight ordeal into a public service – a teaching tool for children and weary parents alike. The premise is simple, if not revolutionary: a whimsical fairy with a plunger wand who teaches young readers about the great mysteries of public restrooms. It's equal parts etiquette manual, survival guide, and cautionary tale, all wrapped in glitter and moral hygiene.

When I presented the idea to my publisher, she stared at me the way one might regard a man proposing Beenie Babies as a retirement plan. Finally, she said, "It fills a niche no one asked for. But it might sell."

Daisy was furious she didn't star in it. Ralph wanted a cameo as a track coach in the chapter on "Sprinting to the Stall." Deaf Hugh begged to appear as a hand dryer maestro. I told them all no – The Tinkle Fairy was a solo act.

When the manuscript finally went to print, the cover showed a dainty fairy hovering over a golden toilet seat, wand aloft, wings sparkling, and just the faintest halo of bathroom steam behind her. Tasteful. Almost.

For the first time, Pee O'Clock wasn't just my private running joke. It was going public – immortalized in glossy paper, questionable dignity, and a marketing campaign that included glow-in-the-dark bookmarks.

Some writers leave behind great novels. I leave behind flushable wisdom.

THE BOOK LAUNCH

The signing took place in a downtown bookstore. They put me at a folding table wedged between the children's section and the sign for the restrooms. Placement, I suspect, was intentional.

The manager decorated the store with balloons and a giant cardboard cutout of the Tinkle Fairy, smiling with unnerving confidence. I sat behind the table in my official author uniform: sport coat over T-shirt, no socks, and a grin that said, Yes, this is my life now.

Children arrived in giggling clusters, dragging suspicious parents. "Is this the pee man?" one whispered. A mother muttered, "We'll see if this is appropriate," before buying two copies. My wife sat in the back, arms crossed, sighing audibly. My kids filmed the whole thing, no doubt planning to upload it with the caption #DadHasLostItEvenMore.

I signed books with inscriptions like:

To Elmer: May your aim be true, your adventures be magical, and your shoes stay splash-free.

To Tyler: Aim carefully. Flush the Cheerios when finished, even if you missed breakfast.

To Tony: To a young hero learning the ancient art of aiming—keep practicing!

During the storytime reading, I recited Chapter Three: "The Tinkle Fairy Visits Niagara Falls: When Nature Calls by Nature's Wonder." The kids howled. The parents squirmed. The bookstore manager called her insurance company.

But I looked up and caught my wife's eye. She was still shaking her head, but this time, she was smiling. Against all odds, this ridiculous little book had gathered people together.

STORY TIME WITH THE TINKLE FAIRY

Bookstores smell like paper and possibility. On the day of my first public reading of *The Tinkle Fairy's Guide to Ready-Aim-Fire*, it also smelled like trouble.

I arrived early, armed with a box of books, a mug of caffeinated courage, and the kind of nervous energy usually reserved for dental appointments. A small stage had been set up in the children's corner, right between Goodnight Moon and a stack of plush llamas wearing sunglasses. A rainbow carpet invited kids to plop down in front. Their parents hovered behind them, smiling uncertainly, as though they weren't entirely sure what they'd signed up for.

"Good morning, everyone! Today we're going to meet the Tinkle Fairy – a magical friend who helps children find bathrooms and… I paused for dramatic effect, …teaches little boys how to aim."

The reaction was instantaneous.

The kids exploded into laughter, the kind of high-pitched giggles that ricochet off walls and echo in memory forever. One boy fell backward on the carpet, clutching his belly, while another whispered to his friend, "He said pee!"

The parents, on the other hand, blushed crimson. Some smiled bravely. Others pretended to suddenly become very interested in the plush llama display. One dad coughed into his hand like he'd swallowed a golf ball.

I pressed on, reading the rhymes with all the solemnity of Shakespeare:

"Eyes on the target, feet on the floor,
Flush when you're finished, and don't splash the door."

More giggles. One little girl yelled, "My brother ALWAYS misses!" which earned a sympathetic groan from every mother in the room.

I turned the page.

"When accidents happen– oh yes, they do–
The Tinkle Fairy says, 'It's okay! I believe in you.'"

This time the parents softened. A few even nodded. Because hidden beneath the giggles and embarrassment was the universal truth: every child struggles, and every parent prays for less laundry.

By the end, the kids were chanting, "Tinkle Fairy! Tinkle Fairy!" while the parents shuffled in line for signed copies, torn between mortification and gratitude. I signed books with a flourish, adding the occasional doodle of a fairy with a plunger wand.

When it was over, I packed up, exhausted but elated. My first reading had been chaotic, hilarious, and entirely on brand.

The Tinkle Fairy had made her debut. And judging from the laughter, blushes, questions, and one kid proudly shouting, "I'm gonna aim better now!", I was already making the world a cleaner place.

Epilogue: The Luckiest Man

I don't know what tomorrow's pre-dawn will bring. Maybe another long-lost utensil will stagger in with a story about Vegas. Maybe Ralph will finally get his Nike endorsement. Maybe Daisy will succeed.

But I do know this: when the rest of the world wakes up and starts texting, emailing, and pretending to be rational, I'll already have lived a whole second life with my early morning family.

And maybe, just maybe, that's the real secret of Zero Dark Thirty-it's the time when the weirdos come out, sip coffee, and remind me that survival is just another word for finding good company in the dark.

The world may see madness. My family may roll their eyes, but every dawn, I rise, shuffle, flush, brew, and scribble. I blur daydreams with city skylines, children's rhymes with survival rituals.

During a book reading in a kindergarten class, a little boy raised his hand and asked, "Since you wrote a book, are you rich now?"

I smiled and said, "I'm rich in new friends like you."

He thought for half a second and fired back, "Okay… but do you own a jet ski?"

When I said no, he shrugged and declared, "Then nope. Not rich."

I've been called eccentric, ridiculous, delusional, and don't own a jet ski. Maybe all true. But I've also been called an author. And somehow, that's enough.

In the end, Pee O'Clock gave me more than sleepless nights. It gave me a fellowship, a rhythm, and a story worth telling.

And for that, I'm the luckiest man alive.

WILL THE REAL DR. MADDOG PLEASE STAND UP?

Mark "Dr. Maddog" Donnelly, PhD, has worn many hats over the years—newspaper publisher, college professor, branding consultant, community activist, photographer, and author of more than fifty books. But at four in the morning, none of that matters. At Pee O'Clock he is simply another bleary-eyed man navigating the treacherous hallway between bed and bathroom, accompanied by a homicidal cat, a caffeinated spider, and a bragging swizzle stick who insists he once stirred cocktails at the Playboy Club.

The nickname "Dr. Maddog" started as a college joke, later became an email address, eventually a pen name, and now an identity that absolutely refuses to fade. These days it's less about bravado and more about resilience—a reminder that even in life's grayer chapters, there is room for humor, mischief, creative chaos, and a very strong cup of coffee.

A lifelong Buffalonian, Mark writes children's books, Buffalo history, cookbooks, and whatever else wanders into his imagination at zero-dark-thirty.

Although this book roughly mirrors his life, he insists this is fiction and not his autobiography. That will be much smaller, infinitely weirder, and absolutely never written.

Beyond the pre-dawn antics, Dr. Donnelly is an accomplished photographer whose award-winning work has appeared in regional and national exhibitions and major galleries including the Albright-Knox Art Gallery, Burchfield Penney Art Center, Rodman Arts Centre, CEPA Gallery, The NACC, Big Orbit Gallery, Seattle Art Museum, ZGM Gallery, and the Art Gallery of Hamilton.

His books such as ***The Fine Art of Capturing Buffalo, Frozen Assets, Statuesque Buffalo, Shovel Ready City, Buffalo Plot Holes, Celebrating Buffalo's Waterfront, Fluid Connections, and A City Built by Giants***–capture the spirit, grit, and resiliency of Buffalo and the Niagara Frontier.

He lives in Buffalo, New York, with his bride, Princess Laura–the real hero of this story–and an ever-growing cast of kitchen companions who may or may not actually exist. Together they endure Pee O'Clock, judge his creative choices, and ensure he never runs out of material.

So, will the real Dr. Maddog please stand up?

No. He's sitting down with another cup of coffee.

And he's perfectly fine with that.

9 781956 688610